THE WITCH WHO WAS AFRAID OF WITCHES

by Alice Low

Pictures by
Karen Gundersheimer

 A Children's Choice® Book Club Edition from Macmillan Book Clubs, Inc.

THIS BOOK BELONGS
TO

children's
choice®

For W. K. II

Wendy was the youngest witch in her family.

She had the weakest witch power. And she was afraid of witches. Older, bossy, mean witches like her two sisters.

Her oldest sister *knew* everything.

She knew where
to get the best
sassafras wood
for broomsticks.

She knew where
to get the best
frogs' tongues for
witches' brew.

And she knew where
to get the best
books for
witches' spells.

"Take me with you," Wendy begged when her oldest sister was going to the sassafras grove.

But her oldest sister always said, "You're too young. You don't even have the right kind of wood in your broomstick. No wonder you can hardly take off. You'll never learn. Really, Wendy, you don't know anything."

Wendy wanted to say, "Of course I don't. How can I learn if you won't show me?"

But she was afraid to talk back to her oldest sister.

Her middle sister knew how
to *do* everything best.

She could fly the fastest
of any witch in the valley.

She could cackle the loudest.
When she cackled "*Heh, heh, heh.
I'll get you,*" she really got you.

And she could say the spells in the most frightening voice, to make them work the best.

"Teach me how to say spells in that frightening voice," Wendy begged.

But her middle sister always said, "Really, Wendy, your voice is too weak. You don't even know how to cackle."

Wendy didn't even try to learn the spells. What good would it do if she didn't have a frightening voice?

At night, her sisters had parties.

Wendy would sit at the top of the stairs, listening to the loud cackles of witch laughter. How she wished she could join in!

When one of her sisters saw her she would shout, "Spying, eh? Off with you. It's past your bedtime."

And Wendy would creep into her cold bed, hugging her broomstick.

She was afraid of the dark. Afraid of witches.

Sometimes she tried to make up a spell to put on her sisters.

But she couldn't think of anything. She needed her sisters to tell her the right words.

"At least I have *you*," she said to her broomstick. "You give me a little witch power."

Then, the day before Halloween, she lost her broomstick.

Neither of her sisters would give her another. "Serves you right," they said.

She felt lost without it. Now she had no witch power at all.

On Halloween night, her sisters said, "We are going to the city where there are more people to scare."

"Take me with you," Wendy said. "Please."

"Really, Wendy, how can you come with us when you have no broomstick?" her oldest sister said.

"Can't I ride with you on yours?" Wendy asked.

"Of course not. You would make it too heavy. Stay here, and don't let anyone in. All those trick-or-treaters eat our candy and squirt shaving cream on the rug. Remember, don't let them in."

Wendy wasn't afraid of trick-or-treaters. She was much more afraid of witches.

"Turn off the lights, lock the door, and put out the fire," her oldest sister said. "It will look like nobody is home."

Wendy did as they said.

Then she sat in the dark, shivering. If only she had her broomstick for company.

Soon there was a knock on the door.

"Trick or treat," shouted a voice.
Wendy opened the window and
called out, "There's nobody home."

"You're home," said a small
ghost on the doorstep.
"Well, I'm nobody,"
Wendy said.
"Is that what you are
for Halloween?"
asked the ghost.

"Are you nobody?"

"Yes," Wendy said.
"But I'm dressed
as a witch."

"Well, why don't you come trick-or-treating with me?" asked the ghost. "My best friend, Billy, went trick-or-treating with his other best friend, who doesn't like me. Let's follow them and scare them."

"That sounds good to me," Wendy said. "Though I'm not very good at scaring people. Mostly, *I'm* scared of witches."

"Oh, you'll catch on," said the ghost. "You just go woo, woo, woo."

"That's how *ghosts* go," Wendy said. "Witches cackle. Like this. *Heh, heh, heh. I'll get you.*"

"Very good," said the ghost. "You sound like a real witch."

"Do I?" Wendy said. "I never thought I could cackle before. But I can't be a real witch without a broomstick. I lost mine."

"Oh, if that's all you need, we have an old one at home. Come on."

They walked up a long path to the ghost's house.

The ghost's mother gave Wendy hot chocolate and a candied apple and a broomstick.

Wendy thought it would be nice to stay there all evening, instead of flying around scaring people.

But the ghost said, "Get on. Let's see you ride."

"I'm not any good at riding broomsticks," Wendy said, afraid to try. "I have no witch power."

"Take the broomstick anyway," said the ghost.

So Wendy took the broomstick, but she didn't sit on it. This old kitchen broomstick wouldn't give her any witch power.

"Go on," said the ghost. "Sit on it. It's fun."

"Okay," Wendy said. After all, the ghost didn't expect her to do anything but pretend and have fun.

She sat on the broomstick and said, *"Heh, heh, heh. I'll get you."* Then she gave a little jump.

She took off so fast she hit the ceiling and fell down.

The ghost was amazed. So was the ghost's mother.
"That must be a magic broomstick," said the ghost.
"Here, let me try it."

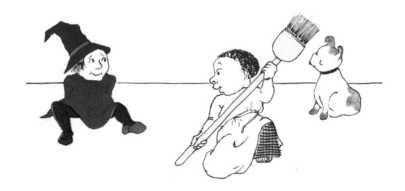

The ghost got on and said, "Heh, heh, heh. I'll get
you." Then he gave a little jump.
But nothing happened.
"Darn it. It doesn't work," said the ghost.

"I'll try it," said the ghost's mother.

She sat on it and cackled and gave a little jump.

But nothing happened again.

They were both very disappointed.

"I'll try it again," Wendy said.

Again, she took off easily. But this time, she zoomed around and around before she landed.

"I guess I do have a little witch power," she said.

"I never thought so before. Except I don't know any spells."

"Then make one up," said the ghost. "You're magic."

That made a really good spell pop into Wendy's head. She said it, in a frightening voice.

Frogs and lizards
Toads and newts
Rubbers, raincoats
Hiking boots.
Turn this ghost
Into a witch.
Presto, change-o
Make a switch.

The ghost's robes turned black.

"Great!" said the ghost. "I wanted to be a witch, but we didn't have any black sheets. But I need a pointed hat."

"Oh, that's easy," Wendy said. "I don't even have to think about that one."

Stew and brew
And cat and bat.
Give this witch
A pointed hat.

"Great!" said the new witch, touching the pointed hat on his head. "Now let's fly out the window."

"Be careful," said the new witch's mother. "Don't fly too fast."

"We won't," they called
from the broomstick
as they flew out,
with Wendy steering.

First they swooped over
trees and made the leaves fall off.

Next they swooped over cars
and scared the drivers.

Then they swooped into
the party where Billy
and his best friend were,
ducking for apples.

Billy and his best friend were so scared, they ran
home crying.

When the clock struck
midnight, Wendy said,
"I'd better fly you home."

"I want to come home with you
and keep on being a witch,"
said the new witch.
"You *are* a real witch,
aren't you?"

"Yes, I am a real witch," Wendy said. "With my own witch power. I just found that out, and you helped. But I have to turn you back into a ghost and take you home. Your mother would miss you."

Broiled figs
And toasted toast.
Turn this witch
Back to a ghost.

The new witch became a ghost again, in his own kitchen.

The ghost's mother let Wendy keep the broomstick.
"Thanks a lot," Wendy said. "See you next Halloween."

And she flew home
and went to sleep
without worrying
about witches.
She wasn't afraid
of witches any more.

When she woke up, her sisters weren't home and it was still dark outside.

"It's far too late for them to be out," Wendy thought. "They may be older, but they have no sense. I'll have to teach them a thing or two."

She took her time making up two spells, one for each sister. They weren't as fancy as the spells her oldest sister found in books. But she knew they had special power because they were her own.

Snakes and cakes
And pumpkin pie.
Oldest sister
You can't fly.

Salt and pepper,
Bouncing ball.
Middle sister
You will fall.

"Oh dear," she thought, after she said the spells, "I forgot to say them in a really frightening voice. Putting spells on my sisters will take the strongest witch power. I hope they work."

An hour later, her sisters came limping home.

Her spells had worked, even though she had used her own voice.

"It was the strangest thing," her oldest sister said. "All of a sudden I couldn't take off. My broomstick was too heavy."

"I took off," her middle sister said. "But the wind blew my broomstick away, and I fell down."

"My broomstick blew away too," her oldest sister said. "We had to walk home. Ow, my feet hurt."

"I feel funny all over," her middle sister said. "As though I'd lost my witch power. Now I know how *you* feel without your broomstick."

"Oh, that's over now," Wendy said. "I found a pretty good broomstick."

"That's just an old kitchen broomstick," her oldest sister said.

"Well, it works," Wendy said. "For me."

"It couldn't possibly," her oldest sister said.

She got on, but she couldn't take off. "I knew it was no good," she said.

Her middle sister got on, but she couldn't take off either.

Then Wendy got on.
She said, *"Heh, heh, heh. I'll get you,"* in her own voice. Then she gave a little jump.
She took off fast, zoomed out the window and

back in, and landed in front of her sisters. She had
flown faster than they ever had.

"How can it be?" her oldest sister said. "I thought I
knew everything. That broomstick isn't even made of
sassafras."

"How can it be?" her middle sister said. "I thought I
knew how to do everything best. And she didn't even
use a frightening voice."

Wendy felt sorry for her sisters.

"You're probably overtired," she said. "Get a good
sleep, and tomorrow you'll be able to fly."

In bed, she made up two spells to take the spells *off*
her sisters.

Oldest sister
You can fly.
All you have to do
Is try.

Middle sister
Flying's fun.
The spell I made
Is now undone.

The next day they went to the sassafras grove to cut
two sticks for brooms.

Wendy's oldest sister looked a long time before she was satisfied.

"This is the best," she said, tying some reeds on to the end of the stick. "Now I'll be able to fly again."

And she did.

Her middle sister found another.

She sat on it and said, *"Mumble, mumble, tumble, tumble,"* in a frightening voice. "Now I'll be able to fly again."

And she did.

Wendy took off too, on her old kitchen broomstick.

She never told them about the spells she had put on them and taken off them.

It was enough to know that her oldest sister thought she knew everything, but didn't.

And that her middle sister thought she knew how to do everything best, but didn't.

And she never told them that she had found her own special witch power. She didn't have to.

They knew she was different.

And they treated her differently. Just like one of them.